OFF WE GO...

The Country Adventure

'Hey!' yelled Michelle. 'Hey!
There's a wild animal in the garden.'

The wild animal was Henry, the cow, who was mooching around to find out all about the new visitor. The visitor was Michelle, down from Dublin for the first time to stay with her country cousins Sinéad and Dara.

In her shiny new red wellies, Michelle sets out to explore the strange ways of country people. She has a lot to learn – but then she has her knowledgeable cousin Sinéad to teach her, and what could be better than that?

In THE DUBLIN ADVENTURE Sinéad and Dara visit Michelle's home to learn about city life.

Siobhán Parkinson

This is Siobhán's second book. Her first, *The Dublin Adventure*, tells the story of the first visit by Sinéad and Dara to Dublin, where they meet their cousin Michelle for the first time. In this book it is Michelle's turn to visit them. Both books belong to the **Off We Go . . .** series.

Siobhán has studied English literature, and spent several years working as an editor in the publishing industry. She now writes training materials for a company which produces training software. Her primary interests are reading and writing.

She lives in Dublin with her husband Roger Bennett and their son Matthew. They do not divide their time between Dublin and Tuscany, though that is their ambition.

To Karyn (of Lismore)
and Kristo (of Shawbrook)

OFF WE GO...

The
COUNTRY
Adventure

Siobhán Parkinson

Illustrated by

Cathy Henderson

THE O'BRIEN PRESS

DUBLIN

First published 1992 by The O'Brien Press Ltd.,
20 Victoria Road, Dublin 6, Ireland.

10 9 8 7 6 5 4 3 2 1
British Library Cataloguing-in-publication Data
Parkinson, Siobhan
Country Adventure. - (Off We Go! Series; No. 2)
I. Title II. Henderson, Cathy III. Series
823.914 [J]

ISBN 0-86278-296-1

The O'Brien Press receives assistance from The Arts
Council/An Chomhairle Ealaíon

Cover design and illustration: Cathy Henderson
Typesetting, layout and design: The O'Brien Press
Printing: The Guernsey Press Co. Ltd., Channel Islands

ONE

*In which Michelle goes to the country
and the adventure begins*

Michelle was going on her holidays to visit her country cousins.

Michelle knows that in the country it's all green and trees and you have to watch out for wild animals like cows and sheep, who would eat you if they got half a chance.

Also, the people in the country are a bit peculiar. They don't have electricity or running water in their houses and most of them speak Irish and at night they sit around the turf fire

and have *céilís* and tell stories about Fionn mac Cumhail and discuss ringworm and liver-fluke.

Michelle was a bit worried about all this, because her Irish is not as good as it should be, and she only likes wild animals in cages.

But Michelle's mother said she would take a few days off work and go to the country with her, so she wouldn't be too lonely and scared.

In fact, her mother went one better than that. She borrowed a car from a friend of hers, so they were able to travel in style.

Off they set and, sure enough, it wasn't long before they were in the country.

It started looking very green and wild around about Maynooth, and by the time they got to Kilcock, Michelle was beginning to think they must be nearly there.

'Not at all,' her mother said, disappointingly, 'sure we're only just beyond the Pale!'

Now, Michelle has never heard of the Pale. But she is pretty smart, and when somebody mentions something in Capital Letters, like the Pale or the Famine or the Land League, she knows to keep her mouth shut and not let on she doesn't know her history.

(Most people can recognise Capital Letters when they are written down. But it takes a very clever person indeed to notice them when they are only spoken.)

'Well, is it nearly lunchtime, then?' asked Michelle.

'No,' said her mother.

It was the sort of 'No' that really means 'And don't ask any more questions,' so Michelle didn't.

Instead she looked out the window at more fields and more wild animals and more hedges and ditches and trees and no people or shops or interesting things at all.

Michelle thought she was going to die of boredom.

She listened to the car radio, and she counted all the red cars and then she counted all the cars with Dublin registration plates.

Then she watched out for round road signs and after that for diamond-shaped ones, and then she tried to work out how many miles 350 kilometres is. (It worked out at 1534 miles, so we won't say anything about Michelle and sums.)

But at long, long last, just when Michelle thought they must be nearly at the end of the world, they arrived in Inishbeg.

Sinéad and Dara had been sitting on the doorstep for the last hour waiting for Michelle to arrive.

But when they saw their Dublin cousin getting out of the car, they suddenly felt all shy, and Dara ran into the house, pretending he was going to call his mother.

9

Aunty Kathleen gave Sinéad a big hug. (Sinéad and Dara call Michelle's mother 'Aunty Kathleen', because she is so much older than them, but really she is their cousin. This makes Michelle a distant sort of cousin.)

'Did you have a nice journey?' asked Sinéad politely, because Sinéad is a very polite little girl.

'Yes, thank you, we had a lovely drive,' said Aunty Kathleen, who is a very polite woman.

'No,' said Michelle at the same time. 'It was really boring. *Dead* boring. Absolutely *desperate*.'

Sinéad smiled. Michelle hadn't changed much since Sinéad and Dara had been to Michelle's house in Dublin last summer.

Sinéad took Michelle off to see the girls' bedroom, while her father and mother and Aunty Kathleen had a cup of tea in the kitchen.

'Why do you sleep downstairs?' asked Michelle.

'Because we haven't got any upstairs,' explained Sinéad.

'Oh,' said Michelle. 'Is this a cottage, so?'

'Well, it's a bungalow,' said Sinéad.

'Same thing,' said Michelle, kicking off her shoes and bouncing on the bed.

'Hey!' she yelled as she bounced past the window. 'Hey! There's a wild animal in the garden.'

Sinéad pulled back the net curtain and peered out, hoping to see something interesting like a squirrel or an otter.

'That's not a wild animal,' she said. 'That's Henry.'

'Of course he's wild!' shouted Michelle. 'He isn't on a lead, is he?'

'You can't put a cow on a lead,' giggled Sinéad, 'and she isn't a *him*, she's a *her*.'

'Well, why is he called Henry if he's a her?' asked Michelle, glaring at Henry and holding a

pillow up to protect herself in case the cow came leaping in the window.

'Short for Henrietta, of course,' said Sinéad, opening the window.

'Don't!' screeched Michelle. 'He'll bite you! He'll EAT you!'

'Don't be ridiculous!' said Sinéad, patting Henry's head, which by now was resting on the windowsill. 'Cows are vegetarians.'

'Vegetarians!' yelped Michelle. 'What's that got to do with it? I don't care what religion he is. It won't stop him biting you.'

Sinéad bent over and whispered in Henry's ear: 'Don't mind her. She's only down from Dublin.'

'Moo,' said Henry comfortably, and nuzzled her head a bit further in the window.

'Eeek!' squealed Michelle. 'He's slobbering all down the wallpaper. Your mother'll kill you, Sinéad. Oh, Sinéad, shut the window before he eats the curtains!'

'I suppose I'd better go and put her out,' sighed Sinéad. 'My dad doesn't like her walking on the lawn.'

'I'm not surprised your dad doesn't like him,' said Michelle.

And off Sinéad went to put Henrietta back in her field. Not a very good start, she thought to herself. Michelle has a few things to learn about life in the country.

Which is certainly true, but then, she has Sinéad to teach her, and Sinéad is sure to make a good job of it.

TWO

In which Michelle makes a friend

The three children were having breakfast together next morning and still feeling a bit shy and wondering what to do next.

'Why don't you take Michelle to see the maternity hospital?' suggested Sinéad and Dara's father, whose name is Uncle Seán. (Or at least, he is Michelle's Uncle Seán.)

'I don't really think I want to see a hospital, thank you,' said Michelle nervously.

'Oh, it's not really a hospital,' explained Sinéad. 'That's just what Dad calls the lambing shed.'

Michelle didn't know what a lambing shed was, but she didn't want to look foolish, so she didn't ask.

After breakfast, they all put on their wellingtons and their warm jackets and off they went across the yard to the lambing shed. (Michelle had nice shiny red boots that she got specially for the country. Sinéad and Dara only had ordinary black ones.)

'I thought sheep lived in fields,' said Michelle, when she saw that the shed was full of sheep and straw and baa-ing and maa-ing noises and a sharpish sort of smell.

'Mostly they do,' said Dara. 'They're just in here for the lambing.'

'These ones here are ewes,' explained Sinéad.

'Yous?' repeated Michelle, puzzled, and looking around to see who else Sinéad thought was there.

'Not yous meaning ye; ewes meaning she-sheep,' said Sinéad patiently.

'She-sheep?' asked Michelle. 'Have you suddenly got a stammer, Sinéad?'

'No,' said Sinéad, 'I'm just trying to explain to you that ewes are she-sheep.'

'Who are you calling sheep?' said Michelle in a cross voice.

Sinéad started to look cross herself.

'It's all right,' said Michelle quickly. 'I'm only joking. I know what you mean. Ewes are she-sheep. Oops! Now I've got a stammer. It must be catching!'

'Those ones there haven't had their lambs yet,' said Sinéad. 'Come and look over here where the new lambs are with their mothers.'

The lambing shed was divided up into lots of little bedrooms, made of bales of straw.

You could look over the bales into each cubicle and in nearly every one there was a ewe with one or two or sometimes even three lambs.

Some had white faces and some had black. Some had very long wobbly legs and some had shorter, stubbier ones. Some were quite big and some were tiny. Even lambs that were brothers and sisters often looked quite unalike.

Very bravely, Michelle put out her hand to pat one. It felt quite tough and knobbly, not a bit soft and fluffy like you'd imagine.

The mother sheep bleated anxiously and shuffled about a bit, glaring at Michelle.

'OK, OK,' said Michelle. 'I'm not going to eat it. Not today anyway.' And she took her hand away.

Just then, the children noticed that one ewe was lying down in a corner of her little bedroom with a sort of a frown on her face, as if she was concentrating very hard on something.

She didn't take any notice of Dara, even when he hung right over the side of the bale of straw, which is very unusual for a sheep, who are rather curious creatures as a rule. This sheep looked as if she had more important things to think about than a small boy.

'Uh-oh,' said Sinéad. 'Better call Mam or Dad, Dara. Michelle and I'll stay with her.'

'Will we?' said Michelle, as Dara scampered off to find a grown-up. 'Why?' she asked. 'He doesn't look as if he wants company.'

'There, there,' Sinéad was saying to the ewe. 'You're grand, you're grand.'

'And it's a *she*, I keep telling you,' she went on, to Michelle. 'When did you last hear of a he having a baby?'

'A baby?' said Michelle. 'Did you say a baby? Is he going to have a baby? Oh, Janey Mac. Oh, oh, oh!'

And she sat down hard on a spare bale of straw.

'What'll we do?' she wailed. 'Will we get the doctor? Oh, Janey Mac!'

Just then Aunty Peggy arrived,

with Dara hot on her heels.

(I don't have to explain that Aunty Peggy is Sinéad and Dara's mother, because you can work that out for yourself.)

'Good girl, Sinéad,' said her mother. 'Well spotted.' And she leapt over the bales of straw to see to the ewe.

Looking back at them over the bales, she said: 'Michelle's gone green. I think you'd better get her into the fresh air.'

'I'm not used to people having babies,' said Michelle, when they got outside. 'Not right under my nose anyway.'

'It's not exactly a baby,' said Dara. 'It's a lamb.'

'But you said a baby, Sinéad,' said Michelle.

'Well, of course I meant a baby sheep, which is a lamb,' said Sinéad. 'Surely you didn't think I meant a *baby*!'

'Not really,' said Michelle. 'Not when I think about it. I suppose I got a bit of a fright.'

'Come on,' said Sinéad. 'I'll race ye over to the Rath Field. It's that next field over there, Michelle, with the whitethorn tree in the middle of it. The tree can be the winning post.'

Sinéad won the race, of course. Her legs are longer than Dara's, so she beat him, and Michelle's boots were new, so she beat her too.

'Have all the fields got names?' asked Michelle, flopping under the tree and taking off her wellies to give her feet an airing.

'Yes,' said Sinéad. 'That's the Ten-Acre Field over there, and that's the Long Paddock, and that's Murray's Field, and that's the Monk's Meadow,' she said, pointing out all the different fields.

'How do you know which one is which?' asked Michelle. 'They're all just fields. They all look the same.'

'But they're all in different places,' said Dara.

'Hmm,' said Michelle. 'That's not much help. Though this field is a bit different all right. It has this nice little hill in the middle of it, and this knobbly little old tree.'

'It's not a hill,' said Dara. 'It's a rath. That means a fairy fort.'

'Oh don't be such a baby, Dara,' scoffed Michelle. 'You don't believe in fairies, do you?'

'Michelle!' said Sinéad in a shocked voice. 'Don't say that! They might hear you!'

'Who?' asked Michelle.

'The Little People.'

'There aren't any little people here, except Dara,' said Michelle. 'And there's only one of him.'

'Much littler than Dara,' said Sinéad in a loud whisper. 'The *Little People!*' and she pointed at the ground they were sitting on.

'Go away out of that, Sinéad,' said Michelle crossly. 'That's a load of rubbish.'

But she stood up all the same and took a good long look around.

'Uncle Dan says it's bad luck to insult them,' said Sinéad.

'Not at all,' said Michelle loudly. But she sat down and put on her shiny red boots again and said: 'Come on. Let's get out of here.'

After that, Sinéad and Dara showed Michelle more of the farm. They saw some older lambs who were big enough to have left the lambing shed and live in the fields with their mothers.

Every now and then, the lambs would all line up together under the wall and suddenly they would sprint off up the field, as if they were having a race. They started all their races in great style, but they never seemed quite sure

where the winning post was, and it all sort of petered out after a bit, with no very clear winner and a lot of losers.

You may already know this, but just in case you don't, I have to explain that sheep (and this includes lambs) are rather stupid animals. They are very well-meaning, of course, they are the best animals ever for producing wool, and they make excellent mothers, but they are very stupid all the same. And this is why lambs can never really organise their races.

Pretty soon, the children began to get that lunch-time feeling, so they left the funny, stupid lambs to their chaotic races and set off towards the house.

When the children got back to the house, there were Aunty Kathleen, Uncle Seán and Aunty Peggy, just about to sit down to the table.

'You kids have great internal clocks,' said Uncle Seán, pouring out three more bowls of soup.

'What's an infernal crock?' asked Dara.

'Oh,' said his father, 'it's a fancy way of saying you'd eat us out of house and home if we weren't careful.'

'Baa!' said somebody.

'What?' said Dara.

'Baa!' said somebody again.

'That's what I thought you said,' said Dara, looking around to see where the sound was coming from.

And what do you think!

There beside the range (which is a kind of large cooker people often have in their kitchens in the country) was a cardboard box, and inside the cardboard box was ... a tiny little new-born lamb.

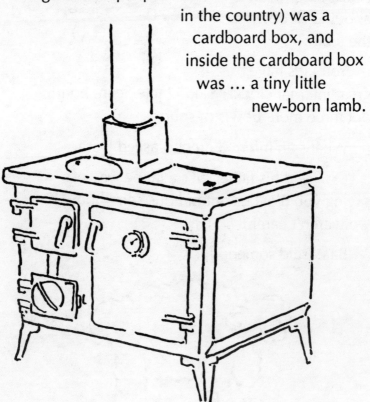

'That ewe you called me to this morning had three lambs,' explained Aunty Peggy. 'Two of them are grand healthy fellows, but this little lad here is a bit on the small side and I don't think the mother has all that much milk, so I thought I'd make a pet of him.'

'A pet!' said Michelle in astonishment. 'A pet lamb! I never heard of a pet lamb before!'

And she went straight over to the box to have a good look at the little lamb.

'What'll we call him?' she asked.

'Well, we usually call them Larry,' said Uncle Seán.

'Usually!' said Michelle. 'Do you often have pet lambs?'

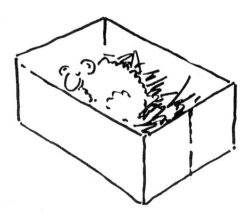

'Oh yes,' said Uncle Seán. 'Most years we have a few. Then we call them Larry One, Larry Two, Larry Three and so on.'

'If you like, Michelle,' said Aunty Peggy, 'you can feed Larry after lunch.'

'Feed him?' asked Michelle. 'You mean put his food in a little dish for him, like feeding a dog?'

'No, no,' said Aunty Peggy. 'Larry's too small for solid food. We feed our pet lambs with a bottle.'

'Like a baby!' said Michelle, astonished again.

Michelle thought country people were definitely a bit strange. They didn't seem to talk Irish as much as she'd expected, or have *céilís*, but they kept pet lambs in cardboard boxes and fed them with a baby's bottle, they let cows stick their heads in the window, and they made straw bedrooms for ewes, and, craziest of all, they imagined they had fairies in the fields.

But she loved feeding Larry.

He wriggled and squirmed when she held him, and in the end Aunty Peggy had to hold him while Michelle held the bottle for him. Then he tried to swallow the bottle and all, and all the time he was making frantic little baa-ing and sucking noises. When he had finished his bottle, there was milk everywhere – little puddles in his box, warm splotches all over Michelle's clothes, even trickles of it over her knees.

But Larry was the happiest lamb in Ireland.

And Michelle, though damp, was beginning to think that maybe wild animals weren't so bad after all.

THREE

In which the children hear more about the fairies and
Uncle Dan shows them the parlour

One afternoon, Sinéad suggested that Michelle might like to visit Uncle Dan.

Michelle thought that was a good idea, so the children set off across the fields to Uncle Dan's house, which is not far away.

'Oh look!' said Michelle, as they walked up the little boreen that led to Uncle Dan's house. 'A proper farmhouse!'

'What do you mean "proper"?' asked Sinéad.

'Well, it's got those cloudy sort of walls and hay on the roof,' said Michelle.

The walls of Uncle Dan's house do indeed look for all the world like clouds that have settled on the ground – white and puffy.

'That's not hay on the roof,' Sinéad pointed out. 'It's straw.'

'Same thing,' said Michelle.

Sinéad looked at Dara, and Dara looked at Sinéad, and they both shrugged their shoulders. Their city cousin doesn't know as much as she thinks she knows.

'Anyway, it's called a thatch,' said Sinéad.

'Well, I know *that*,' said Michelle indignantly.

Just then, one of Uncle Dan's hens came bowing and pecking by, hoping that the children had brought something nice to eat.

'Oh, shoo off,' said Sinéad crossly, and she made a sort of a swooping movement with her hands.

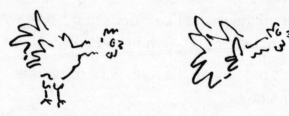

And sure enough, the hen went whooshing away with a panicky little run and a mad flap of wings, and she went circling around in a corner of the yard muttering and clucking to herself in an offended sort of way.

'He understood you,' said Michelle admiringly.

'Well, of course she did,' said Sinéad, peering over the half-door to see if Uncle Dan was about.

And there he was, slumped in a chair with the newspaper opened over his face. He was breathing deeply, and every time he breathed out the newspaper gave a whistly sort of a little flutter and every time he breathed in it sort of lay down again with a sigh.

The children opened the door and went in and made loud coughing noises so that Uncle Dan would wake up and talk to them.

Now, Uncle Dan doesn't like being woken up from his afternoon nap, because he doesn't like anyone to know that he *has* a nap after lunch. So he spluttered and muttered a bit when he saw the children, but really they knew he was quite glad to see them, because before long, he had found four glasses and a bottle of red lemonade and a packet of Custard Creams and they were all settled in to a nice little afternoon snack.

'We saw Henry again the other day,' said Sinéad. 'I think that old gate of yours must be off its hinges.'

'Could be, could be,' said Uncle Dan. 'Or it could be that Henry heard that Michelle was here and she thought she would go and have a look at her.'

'Is Henry *your* cow?' asked Michelle. 'I thought he was Uncle Seán's and Aunty Peggy's.'

'Yes,' said Uncle Dan. 'I mean no. Or do I? I mean, yes, Henry is mine, and no, she's not Seán's. Sinéad and Dara live on a sheep farm. We're the dairy farmers around here.'

'I thought all farms had cows,' said Michelle.

'Not at all,' said Uncle Dan. 'Sure if all farmers kept cows there'd be far too much milk. We'd be swimmin' in it.'

'Like Cleopatra,' said Sinéad.

'Is that another cow?' asked Michelle.

'No,' said Sinéad. 'But it'd be a nice name for a cow all right. I must keep it in mind.'

'I suppose you do know that milk comes from cows, Michelle,' said Uncle Dan severely. 'I hope you're not one of those city children who thinks it comes in bottles.'

'Well,' said Michelle cautiously, '*our* milk in Dublin comes in cartons.'

'Hmm,' said Uncle Dan. 'Well, it'll soon be milking time and we can take you over to see the milking parlour, and then you'll know all about where milk comes from.'

'Uncle Dan,' said Dara, 'Michelle doesn't believe in the fairies.'

'*What!*' said Uncle Dan. And he jumped up and ran and closed the top part of the half-door.

'They might hear you!' he said. 'They don't like it if you are rude about them.'

'I wasn't being rude,' said Michelle. 'It's just that there aren't any fairies in Dublin.'

'Ah well, Dublin!' said Uncle Dan in a poor-old-Dublin-doesn't-know-any-better sort of voice.

'There's the tooth-fairy though,' went on Michelle, thinking she had better stick up for Dublin. 'The tooth-fairy comes to Dublin kids all right.'

'Well then!' said Uncle Dan. 'There you are!'

'So will you tell us about the fairies?' said Dara.

'Well,' said Uncle Dan, folding up his newspaper in such a businesslike way that the children knew they were in for a chat.

'Well,' he said again. 'The fairies are really people from another world, and another time. They are the spirits of people who lived in Ireland long, long ago. And because they do not really belong to this world, they have no land of their own, and they have no cows or milk or hens or eggs.'

'Spirits don't eat eggs,' said Michelle.

Uncle Dan glared at her.

'So what do they do?' asked Dara.

'Oh,' said Uncle Dan, 'the farming people share their milk and eggs with them. But sometimes people are very mean, and they won't share with the Little People.'

'Do you share with them?' asked Michelle.

'Certainly I do,' said Uncle Dan. 'I know how to behave. I always leave out something for the Little People.'

'What happens if you don't?' asked Dara.

'Well,' said Uncle Dan, 'then the Little People have to steal things.'

'That's not very nice,' sniffed Sinéad.

'Oh,' said Uncle Dan, 'they don't like to steal – but they will if they have to.'

'Tell us about the thorn trees,' begged Sinéad.

'Well,' went on Uncle Dan, 'the fairies always mark the places they live in with a thorny tree – a whitethorn or, as some people call it, a hawthorn tree.

'Now one thing that makes the fairies very cross is if somebody cuts down their tree. That's asking for trouble.

'So sensible farmers never cut down an old whitethorn tree, even if it's in the middle of a field, getting in the way of the tractor and the plough.'

'What would they do to you if you cut their tree down?' asked Michelle.

'Oh, they might make your milk go sour,' said Uncle Dan. 'Or make your hens lay out.'

'What does that mean?' asked Michelle.

'It means they would make your hens lay their eggs in places where you couldn't find them,' said Uncle Dan. 'And then where would you be?'

'Well, you'd be here,' said Michelle. 'But your eggs wouldn't be, I suppose.'

'Exactly,' said Uncle Dan.

Just then they could hear a lot of moo-ing in the distance, and gates being swung open and a dog barking and somebody whistling and then they could hear the shuffle of hooves and more moo-ing and a man's voice shouting 'Hup-hup' (which is a very strange thing to say to cows, when you think about it, but the cows seem to understand it all right).

'That'll be Gerry and Prince bringing home the cows for the evening milking,' said Uncle Dan. 'Let's show Michelle our lovely milking parlour, will we?'

Gerry is Uncle Dan's grown-up son. He lives in a new house near Uncle Dan's and does most of the farm work now. And Prince is his dog.

In the milking parlour, the cows were already lining up, each one in her place, with a little snack in front of her, and Gerry was having a few words in each cow's ear as he put on the milking clusters. Each cow swished her tail in a conversational sort of way when Gerry spoke to her.

'But this is just a shed,' said Michelle, looking around her.

'Just a shed!' snorted Uncle Dan. 'This, my dear young lady, is the finest milking parlour

west of the Shannon. Would you take a look at the technology we have here!'

And he waved his hand at the gleaming computer screen and a clutter of temperature gauges and glass tanks and pistons and gadgets and pipes and trunnions and goodness knows what.

'Well,' said Michelle, 'I'm sure it's very nice machinery. But still you couldn't really call it a parlour. It hasn't even got a carpet.'

'It's not *that* sort of a parlour,' said Sinéad. 'It's for cows, not people.'

Just then, some lovely music started up, drowning out the loud whirring sound of the machinery.

'Ah, Mozart's Piano Concerto No. 21,' said Uncle Dan. 'Henry's favourite.'

'You play music to the *cows*!' shrieked Michelle. She had seen and heard a lot of strange things since she had come to Inishbeg. But this really was the very strangest of all.

'Oh yes,' said Uncle Dan. 'They love it. It helps them to relax and give their milk quickly and easily.'

And to think that Michelle had thought country people didn't even have electricity and here they were with computers and everything that flashed and beeped, and a hi-fi system in the cowshed!

Dusk was starting to draw in when they left the milking parlour, and Uncle Dan told the children that they'd better get off home quickly before it got dark.

So they said goodbye to him and to Gerry and Prince and Henry and the others, and off they scampered across the fields in the gathering grey of the evening.

FOUR

In which Michelle has a friend to sleep

When the children got home from Uncle Dan's, Aunty Peggy said to them: 'Oh good, you're just in time to help. Will you girls mix the batter for the pancakes, please, while I get on with the bread? You can lay the table later, Dara, if you don't mind.'

Well, of course, nobody minded helping in the kitchen when it was pancakes. So they put their aprons on and got down to work.

'Did you say you were going to fry bread?' Michelle asked Aunty Peggy.

'No. Not fry it. Bake it. Or at least, first I have to make the dough and then bake it.'

'You mean, you actually make bread, real bread, like you get in the shops?' asked Michelle in astonishment.

'Yes, real bread,' said Aunty Peggy, as she measured out spoonfuls of white flour into a bowl for the pancakes, and then brown flour into a heap on the kitchen table.

'But no, not a bit like you get in the shops.'

And she sprinkled bread-soda onto the heap of flour. Then she went to the pantry and came back with a big jug. She made a deep dent in the middle of her heap of flour and poured in

some milk. The milk was thick and it made glopping noises as it fell into the flour in big blobs.

'Oh Janey,' said Michelle. 'That's an awful pity! The milk is sour. Now the flour is ruined. What a waste!'

'No,' said Sinéad. 'It's supposed to be sour.'

'Yuck!' said Michelle. 'How could you eat something made of sour milk? Disgusting!'

'Wait and taste it, Michelle,' said Aunty Peggy, mixing the dough and giving it a quick roll to make a nice floury ball. Then she patted it out into a flattish cake and slashed a cross on top of it with a sharp knife.

'Why do you mark it like that?' asked Michelle.

'To help it to cook in the middle,' said Aunty Peggy. 'But some people would tell you it is to keep away the fairies.'

'Do you believe in the fairies, Aunty Peggy?' asked Michelle.

'Well,' said Aunty Peggy, 'I'm sure the cross helps my bread to bake better and sure if it helps to keep away the fairies too, then that's no harm either.'

'Ah, Mam,' said Dara. 'That's not a proper answer.'

'Maybe not, Dara,' said Aunty Peggy. 'But you know there are no proper answers to questions like that.' Which is just the sort of infuriating thing that grown-ups say.

Aunty Peggy put the bread in the oven and closed the oven door.

'What about the fairy rath in the Rath Field?' asked Sinéad. 'That's real, isn't it?'

'Oh yes,' agreed her mother. 'But a rath is probably a place where the ancient Irish buried

their most important people when they died –
kings and queens and chieftains.'

'How long ago was that?' asked Dara.
'Before the Vikings?'

'Oh, way before the Vikings,' said his mother.

'Before Cleopatra?' asked Sinéad.

'Yes,' said Aunty Peggy. 'Before Cleopatra.
Before ancient Rome. Before Christ.'

'Gosh, that's a very long time. Do you think
our rath is really that old?' asked Sinéad.

'Yes, I certainly do,' said her mother. 'So
even if it doesn't belong to the fairies it is still a
very special place.'

'Aunty Peggy,' said Michelle with a grin, 'I
think *you've* been out flattening raths or cutting
down hawthorn trees and annoying the fairies.'

'What makes you think that?' asked her aunt.

'Well, look at that milk you used to make the bread. It was very sour,' said Michelle. 'Uncle Dan said the fairies make the milk go sour on people that are nasty to them!'

'Oh, Michelle!' said Aunty Peggy, and they all laughed.

That night, something woke Michelle up. She wasn't sure what it was. (Perhaps it was her tummy grumbling because of too many pancakes.)

She lay still under the blankets and listened. It wasn't a bit like lying awake in her own house. In Dublin, she could lie in bed and she would always hear traffic whizzing by on the

main road a few streets away. And there was
always a glow of light outside the bedroom
window.

But in the country, when Michelle listened,
all she could hear was the distant bleating of
the occasional sheep and the swish of the trees
in the wind. And there was no comforting glow
of light. Michelle had never seen so much dark
before.

She lay there, looking at all this dark, and
thinking about raths and fairies and thorny trees
and wondering if the rath on the farm was
really the grave of an ancient chief or if maybe
there were fairies in it after all.

She was just thinking to herself that really the
tooth-fairy they had in Dublin was an
altogether nicer sort of creature, when one of
the sounds she could hear in the distance
suddenly seemed to be much closer.

Do you know that scary feeling you sometimes get if you lie awake all by yourself in the dark and think about fairies and stuff?

It sort of creeps up your back and tickles the back of your neck and makes your throat go dry. Well, just imagine getting that feeling in the darkest room you can think of, miles away from your own bedroom. That's just how Michelle felt.

She lay very quiet. Pretty soon, even her own breathing started to sound spooky.

And then she heard the sound again: Baa! Quite plainly. Of course! It wasn't so strange after all to hear a bleating sound in the house. Sure wasn't Larry in the kitchen!

Michelle felt a lot better when she remembered about Larry. But then she began to wonder why he was bleating in the night. She wondered if maybe he was hungry. Or just lonely. She thought she'd better go and have a look.

So she rolled out of bed carefully, so as not to wake Sinéad, and shuffled off up the long narrow passage that led from the bedrooms to the kitchen.

She found the light switch after a lot of muttering and fumbling and when the kitchen light went on, there was poor Larry in the middle of the floor, wobbling on his long spindly legs. He must have managed to get out of his box by the range and then lost his way.

'Poor lamb,' said Michelle to the little creature, who was blinking and bleating and looking very miserable. 'You must be lonely and scared all by yourself in this dark kitchen,' she said to him. 'And to tell you the truth,' she went on, gathering the little thing up into her arms, 'I'm feeling a bit lonely and scared myself.'

Little Larry felt very small and fragile in her arms. His legs were like thin sticks and she could feel his heart beating very fast against his sides. And before she really knew what she was doing, she had elbowed the light off, kicked the door closed and set off back down the corridor to her bedroom – with Larry still in her arms.

In no time at all, Michelle had snuggled back into her bed, with Larry snuffling away beside her, and in two shakes of a lamb's tail she had dropped off to sleep.

Shortly after this, something woke Sinéad. She sat up in bed and listened. She thought she heard a bleating sound. Now, bleating sounds are not very unusual on a sheep farm, but somehow this bleating sound seemed different.

Louder.

That's it. It was louder than the bleating sounds she was used to hearing in the night.

Then she remembered that Larry was in the kitchen.

'Poor old Larry,' she thought. 'I'd better go and check on him.'

So she swung out of bed and slithered into her slippers but she didn't put on the bedroom light because she didn't want to wake Michelle. And so she never noticed, in the dark, that Michelle had a sleeping companion.

Off went Sinéad, down the corridor to the kitchen. She turned on the kitchen light, and there was Larry's box – but there was no sign of Larry. Where could he be?

Well, you and I know where he was, but Sinéad was very puzzled indeed. She looked under the table and under all the chairs, and in the little spaces between the range and the press and between the fridge and the wall, but there was no Larry.

She went over and felt his bed. It was still warm, so she knew he couldn't be gone very long. Then she checked the windows. They were all tightly closed. And she was quite sure the kitchen door had been closed when she came in.

This was very strange. Sinéad sat down at the kitchen table in her pyjamas and wondered what to do next. She thought Larry must have been kidnapped. It was the only explanation. She'd better wake up her mother and father and get them to ring the guards.

Well, you can imagine the commotion there was when Sinéad appeared in her parents' bedroom in the middle of the night. Her mother and father sat up with their hair all sticking out and their eyes very pink and watery looking, and wanted to know what was wrong.

'It's Larry,' sobbed Sinéad. 'He's been stolen!'

'By the fairies, I suppose,' said her mother.

'Oh, do you think that could be it?' asked Sinéad, even more worried now. You could ring the guards if it was just robbers. But there wasn't much you could do about the fairies.

'No,' said her mother. 'I don't really think so at all. Come on, Seán. Let's investigate.'

And so then there were three sleepy people in their pyjamas looking around the kitchen and calling 'Larry!' They looked pretty silly, I can tell you.

Just then, Larry gave a little bleat. But of course it was a far-away sort of bleat, because it was coming from the bedroom.

'Sh!' said Sinéad's father. 'I think I hear him. He's in the house somewhere. Come on.'

And back down the corridor towards the bedroom trooped the three detectives.

'Baa!' said Larry again, obligingly.

'Good heavens!' said Sinéad's mother. 'I think it's coming from your room, Sinéad.'

Which, of course, it was.

Uncle Seán turned on the light, and there was Michelle, still fast asleep, and there was Larry, comfortable but hungry, snuggled in beside her.

'Good grief!' said Aunty Peggy.

'What?' said Michelle sleepily, opening her eyes and blinking.

'Michelle! What on earth are you doing with Larry?' asked Aunty Peggy. 'Has he piddled in the bed? Oh dearie me!'

'Oh,' said Michelle, sitting up. 'I never thought of that. Is he not house-trained?'

'You don't house-train lambs, Michelle,' said Uncle Seán.

'But I thought he was supposed to be a pet,' said Michelle. 'You'll have to house-train him, won't you?'

'No, no, it's not like that,' said Uncle Scán. 'A pet lamb means a lamb that is fed from a bottle by human beings, because its mother isn't able to feed it herself. It doesn't mean that you treat the lamb like a pet dog or cat.'

'Oh,' said Michelle, getting very red in the face, and feeling very stupid indeed, 'I didn't know.'

'Sure of course you didn't know,' said Aunty Peggy gently. 'It's a silly expression really. But you do see, Michelle, that you can't treat a lamb like a pet. After all, it will grow up to be a sheep.'

'And,' said Sinéad, 'you know how stupid sheep can be.'

'About as stupid as me, I suppose,' said Michelle, with a tiny smile.

'It's not stupid to make a mistake, Michelle,' said Aunty Peggy. 'Now, let's get Larry back to the kitchen and you two back to sleep.'

Luckily, Larry hadn't piddled in the bed, so Aunty Peggy tucked Michelle in again and turned off the lights.

'Michelle,' said Sinéad's voice from across the room in the dark, when the grown-ups had left. 'I made a mistake tonight too. I thought the fairies had stolen Larry.'

'Oh Sinéad!' said Michelle with a giggle. 'Aren't we the right pair of eejits.'

FIVE

In which we meet the hens
and something surprising happens

Aunty Peggy had given the children the job of looking after the hens for the holidays.

On Uncle Dan's farm, you may remember, the hens are a bit wild and they scrabble about in the farmyard. But on Sinéad and Dara's farm they live in a little house in a corner of the farmyard, with a hen-run outside it. (A hen-run is a sort of a front garden for a hen-house, with chicken wire around it to keep the hens safe inside.)

When the children went to feed the hens, they would make loud chuck-chuck noises (which are supposed to sound like a mother hen calling her chicks, but really sound just like three children making chuck-chuck noises), and then the hens would know it was breakfast-time.

Then, while the hens were busy scratching around for the food, the three children would go into the hen-house to collect the eggs.

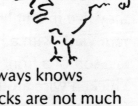

'How come there are all these mother hens and only one cock?' asked Michelle, one morning.

'Well,' said Sinéad, who always knows everything, 'that's because cocks are not much use. They don't lay eggs. So there is no point in keeping a whole lot of them.'

'Well, then, why do you bother to have even the one?' asked Michelle.

'Oh, you have to have a cock,' said Sinéad. 'It's like that with all farm animals. You just keep a few father animals and a whole lot of mothers. That way you get lots of babies.'

'So all the men have lots of wives,' said Michelle.

'Yes,' said Sinéad. 'But all the women have lots of friends.'

The hens never seemed to notice that every morning their eggs disappeared, and they went on day after day merrily laying egg after egg

without once stopping to wonder why they hardly ever had any chicks.

Several mornings in a row, the children collected quite a lot of eggs, and soon there were more eggs than the family could eat. Uncle Seán thought they should each have two fried eggs for breakfast every day until they had eaten them all up, but Sinéad told him that that would be terribly bad for them because eggs are full of cholesterol.

'My, my,' said Aunty Kathleen admiringly. 'What a big word for a little girl.'

Aunty Peggy said she had a much better idea. It would be Easter Sunday very soon, she reminded them. They could boil the eggs and paint and decorate them to make real Easter eggs for their friends.

Michelle looked a bit worried. She said that as far as she knew real Easter eggs were made of chocolate.

Before Sinéad could tell her how bad too much chocolate was for her, Aunty Peggy said: 'Well, of course, we can all have some chocolate eggs. But wouldn't it be nice to decorate real eggs as well?'

The children agreed that it would, so Aunty Peggy boiled some eggs and they all had a great afternoon painting the eggs and sticking glitter and shapes cut out of tinfoil on them.

'Uncle Dan says the sun dances when it rises on Easter Sunday morning,' said Dara, as he stuck a transfer on an egg. 'Do you think it really does?'

'Maybe it does,' said his mother. 'But we've never been up early enough to find out.'

Well, I have to report that nobody in that house was up early enough on Easter Sunday to see the sun dancing in the sky. But even if they had been up in time they would probably have missed it anyway, because the children would have been too busy opening the lovely chocolate eggs they had been given.

Aunty Kathleen and Michelle had brought special eggs from Bewley's in Dublin for Sinéad and Dara, and Michelle got a surprise when she found out that her mother had secretly brought one for her as well.

The eggs had beautiful flower patterns embroidered on them in coloured icing. They were almost as pretty as the real Easter eggs the children had decorated themselves, and they tasted even better.

On Easter Monday morning, the children got up early and went to feed the hens and collect the eggs as usual. Just as they were leaving the hen-house, Michelle had a nice idea.

She had been watching the hens flapping about the hen-run and sometimes taking flying leaps at the sides of the run, as if they wanted to fly off and have adventures. She felt sorry for the poor hens having only their hen-run to play in, so, instead of locking the little gate of the hen-run, she just pushed it across, so that the hens could get out and go for a walk about the farm if they liked.

Sinéad and Dara had gone on ahead because they were looking forward to a delicious slice of their mother's bread for breakfast, so they didn't notice what Michelle was up to and none of the hens seemed to notice either, as they were still busy with their food.

Now, thought Michelle, that'll be nice for them. And off she trotted to catch up with the others.

Late that evening, Uncle Seán came rushing into the kitchen in his farm clothes.

'I need some help,' he said. 'The hens have all got out. The gate to the hen-run is open and there's nothing but straw and feathers in the hen-house.'

So everyone put on their warm jackets and boots and got torches and sticks and off they all went on a hen-hunt in the dark.

'Do you think it's a fox, Dad?' asked Dara as they went.

'No,' said his father. 'A fox couldn't have opened the gate. It has to have been some stupid or bad-minded person. But the thing is, if there are foxes about tonight, those hens don't stand a chance.'

Well, they swung their torches around and shone beams into ditches and hedges and hollows all over the farmyard, but not a hen was in sight.

Suddenly a yell went up from Dara. 'Look in the tree!' he shouted. 'Look in the apple tree!'

They all looked up, and saw dark smudges in the branches of an old apple tree just beyond the farmyard. Some of the smudges were asleep and the others were clucking drowsily, as if they were telling each other bedtime stories.

Everyone laughed at the silly birds who hadn't the sense to realise that their nice warm hen-house was much safer and more comfortable than an apple tree. But they weren't laughing two hours later when, after lots of whooshing and shouting and chasing, they finally got the last reluctant hen into bed.

'I think hot whiskies are what the grown-ups need after that little adventure,' suggested Uncle Seán on the way back to the house. 'And cocoa for the children.'

He was standing at the range, pouring milk into a saucepan for the children's cocoa, when he thought he heard a little cheeping sound.

'I must have chickens on the brain,' he laughed. 'I could have sworn I heard a chick.'

'Well, you can't have,' said Aunty Peggy, who was searching for cloves in the back of the press.

'I think I must have something wrong with my ears then,' said Uncle Seán. 'Because I'm just after hearing it for the second time!'

'There's nothing wrong with your ears, Seán,' said Michelle's mother. 'Unless it's something catching. Because I heard it that time too.'

'Oh, it must be those blessed pipes again,' said Aunty Peggy, knocking irritably at the copper water pipes that went up behind the range.

'There it is again,' said Aunty Kathleen. 'It really does sound remarkably like a newly hatched chick.'

There was a box beside the range. In it was some straw that was left over from when Aunty Peggy made a bed for Larry. Just as Aunty Kathleen spoke, there was a rustling sound in the box. And what do you think peeped out, but a fluffy little yellow head!

'Where did you come from?' Dara asked it.

'Oh my goodness gracious me!' exclaimed Aunty Peggy. 'I've got it!'

'The jar of cloves?' asked Aunty Kathleen.

'No. The explanation!' said Aunty Peggy.

'Do you remember the day I was boiling the eggs for the children to decorate?'

They all remembered, of course.

'Well,' went on Aunty Peggy, 'I had too many eggs to fit in the saucepan, so I put one down in that box of straw. I must have forgotten all about it and left it there.'

'Well,' said Uncle Seán, 'that box of straw must have made a perfect little nest for the egg, nice and soft and warm enough for it to hatch out.'

'Let's call the chick "Cleopatra",' suggested Sinéad, fluffing its furry down with her fingers.

'No,' said Uncle Seán, 'let's call it "Surprise". Because that's exactly what it was.'

Everyone agreed that this was a great name.

The children wanted to make a pet of Surprise.

'Surprise would probably be happier in the hen-house, with the other hens,' said Uncle Seán. 'But I suppose it can stay around the house for a few days anyway.'

'Oh goody!' said the children.

'But we don't want anybody getting any bright ideas about taking it to bed for a cuddle,' said Uncle Seán.

Michelle blushed. Then she burst into tears.

'Oh dear,' said Uncle Seán. 'I'm sorry. I'm very mean to be teasing you. Don't cry now, there's a good girl.'

'It's not ...' sobbed Michelle.

'It's not what?' asked Dara.

'It's not ...' Michelle tried again.

'It's not the teasing that's upsetting you,' suggested Aunty Peggy.

Michelle nodded.

'I'll tell you what,' said Aunty Peggy. 'Here's a hanky. Now cry a bit more if you like. And when you've finished, wipe your eyes and blow your nose, and then tell us what it is.'

Michelle sobbed again, but then she wiped her nose and said: 'It's not the teasing. It's the hens.'

'Ah,' said Uncle Seán, 'now we're getting places. The hens are making Michelle cry.'

'No,' said Michelle, shaking her head and blowing her nose again.

'It's me. I mean ... I mean ... I mean, it was me that left the hen-run gate open.' And she started to sob again.

'Well, well, well,' said Uncle Seán, 'that's nothing to cry about, Michelle. It was a bit silly of course, but it's not the end of the world now, is it?'

'N-n-no,' agreed Michelle. 'I just thought they might like to get out and stretch their wings a bit.'

'And so they did,' said Uncle Seán. 'I think it's very brave of you to have owned up, Michelle.'

'I-i-is it?' asked Michelle.

'Yes,' said Uncle Seán. 'But you know, Michelle, you shouldn't put salt in cocoa.'

'I didn't put salt in the cocoa,' said Michelle, mystified.

'Yes, you did,' said her uncle. 'All those salty tears have been plopping right into your cup, after all the trouble I went to to make it for you.'

And all the children laughed. Even the grown-ups laughed. And they all agreed that they'd never had a better Easter.